SIMPLE SCIENCE
HOW THINGS WORK

Martyn Bramwell
Illustrated by David Mostyn
Designed by Sylvia Tate
Consultants: Alan Ward and Patrick Eve

Contents

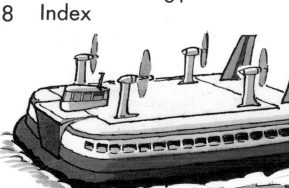

Exploring science

The world is full of machines – from egg beaters and bicycle brakes to bulldozers and space rockets. Learning about how they work is great fun because they all depend on quite simple scientific ideas.

You can see these ideas in action for yourself by doing your own experiments and by making working models. That is why this book is packed full of interesting and surprising things to make and do.

Scientists are always asking questions and searching for the answers. You can do that too. Look around you and try to work out what makes things happen, in the world of nature as well as in the world of man-made machines. Ask lots of questions, and try as many experiments as you can think of. Some work perfectly every time. Others are a bit more tricky. But remember that even the most famous scientists get things wrong sometimes. If an experiment does not work the first time, try it again. That is what scientific experiments are all about.

Home-made pulleys

You will need small pulleys for some of the experiments. You can buy them quite cheaply from most model shops. You can also make them yourself from cotton reels, old toy car wheels, or from cork and card.

Cut the reel   Glue ends together

Peel off tyre

Wire

Card   Cork

'Science corner'

All sorts of odds and ends can come in useful for experiments. Instead of throwing broken toys away, put any useful bits like wheels, springs, motors and fasteners into a box. You could keep another box for such things as plastic containers and bits of tubing, and another box for your tools, paints and glues.

SPRINGS AND THINGS

TOOLS

Force measurers

In some experiments you will want to measure how much 'pull' it takes to make something happen. This is how to make a simple force measuring device.

You will need a fairly strong rubber band, two paper clips, a strip of sticky-backed paper, a bead, a short piece of string, some plasticine and a clear plastic tube. (The sort that toothbrushes are packed in work very well.)

Put the force measurer together like this. Then use the kitchen scales to measure out four lumps of plasticine weighing 100g, 200g, 300g, and 400g. (You will not need them again after the force measurer has been set up.)

PAPER CLIP HANGER

RUBBER BAND

BEAD MARKER

STRIP OF PAPER

STRING

PAPER CLIP HOOK

PLASTIC TUBE

Hang the force measurer up and put a mark on the paper strip opposite the bead. Now hang the 100g weight on the hook and mark the new position of the bead. Do this for each of the other test weights. You can complete the scale by adding extra marks at 25g intervals between the test marks.

25g marks

100g mark

No weight

100g weight

Now, if you attach the measurer to a weight and pull steadily, the position of the bead will show you how many grammes of 'pull' it takes to start the weight moving.

Weight

Good scientists are always **very** careful about safety, especially when doing experiments with sharp tools or anything hot. Take good care, and always ask a grown-up to help when you see this red warning colour.

What goes up usually comes down

When you throw a ball into the air it falls back to Earth. But what makes it do that? You used a force to send the ball up, so some other force must bring it back. That force is called gravity.

Every object has its own force of gravity, from huge planets right down to atoms that are too small even to see. The bigger an object is, the more powerful is its gravitational pull. And the closer you are to a big object the more you can feel that pull. Earth's gravity is very strong. It keeps us all firmly on the ground. Without it we would float off into space.

The story says that Sir Isaac Newton discovered this invisible force when an apple fell on him from a tree.

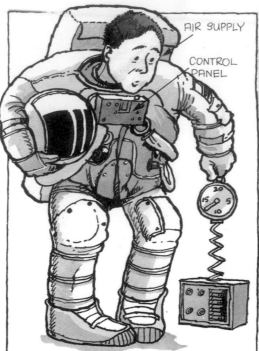

AIR SUPPLY

CONTROL PANEL

The astronaut finds it quite hard to move about on Earth. His spacesuit and life-support backpack weigh as much as 26 kilos on Earth. This man's experiment pack weighs 12 kilos in Earth's gravity.

LIQUID FUEL TANK (700,000 KILOS OF FUEL)

BOOSTER ROCKET

REUSABLE SPACE SHUTTLE

USA

Huge solid-fuel booster rockets and an enormous tank of liquid fuel for the second stage are needed to blast the two-million-kilo space shuttle far enough from Earth for it to escape Earth's gravity.

Which falls faster – a pebble or a paper tissue?

Drop an open tissue and a pebble from the same height. Which hits the ground first? Now try again with the tissue screwed into a tight little ball. What happens?

Gravity tries to make everything fall at the same speed. The open tissue slows down because it has a lot of air trapped under it.

Gravity power

A weight being pulled towards the Earth by gravity can be used as a source of power. Try making this simple model merry-go-round, driven by a falling weight. (When the model spins, watch what happens to the 'chairs'. We will come to this again later.)

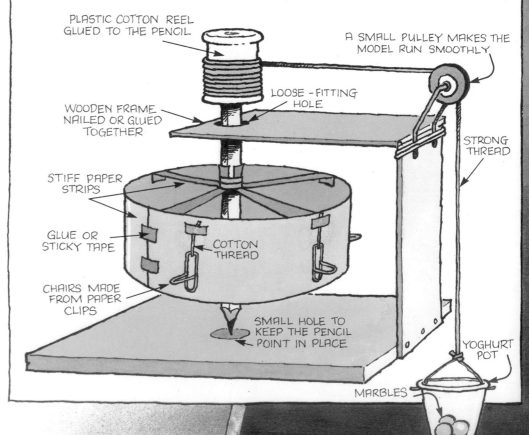

PLASTIC COTTON REEL GLUED TO THE PENCIL

A SMALL PULLEY MAKES THE MODEL RUN SMOOTHLY

LOOSE – FITTING HOLE

WOODEN FRAME NAILED OR GLUED TOGETHER

STRONG THREAD

STIFF PAPER STRIPS

GLUE OR STICKY TAPE

COTTON THREAD

CHAIRS MADE FROM PAPER CLIPS

SMALL HOLE TO KEEP THE PENCIL POINT IN PLACE

YOGHURT POT

MARBLES

As the astronauts travel away from Earth, the pull of Earth's gravity gets weaker. Far out in space it can hardly be felt at all. The scientists float about — almost weightless.

Because the Moon is very much smaller than Earth, gravity there is much weaker. This crewman's experiment pack now weighs only 2 kilos, one-sixth of its weight on Earth.

SAFETY LINE

Outside the space-lab an astronaut drifts in a world where there is no 'up' or 'down'. How much do you think his experiment pack weighs now?

MOON BUGGY

Gravity at work

You can see gravity at work all around you. It can be used to do heavy jobs like breaking stones or driving posts into the ground. It makes liquids flow downhill without needing pumps. And a weight on a string always hangs straight down, so it can be used to check that things are perfectly upright.

The bricklayer uses a 'plumb line' to check that his wall is not leaning.

The pull of gravity helps the joiner's hammer do its job.

The pile-driver keeps lifting and dropping a large weight to ram steel sheets into the ground.

Gravity makes the ready-mixed concrete flow down the chute.

Stopping and starting

Have you noticed how people standing on a bus lurch forward when the driver brakes, then sway backwards when the bus pulls away from the bus stop or traffic lights? It is all due to something called inertia. If an object is

moving, inertia tries to keep it moving. That is why cars need plenty of room to stop. If an object is standing still, inertia tries to keep it still. That is why it takes so much pushing to move a broken-down car.

Stopping safely
In a car crash, the car stops very quickly but inertia tries to keep the passengers moving. Seat belts catch the passengers and stop them being thrown against the windscreen.

Fool your friends with inertia tricks

Question: Can you put the coin in the glass without touching either of them?

Answer: Flick the card sharply with your finger. Inertia keeps the coin still for the split second it takes for the card to fly clear.

Question: Can you take the bottom coin away without moving the pile?

Answer: Knock the bottom coin out of the pile with the blunt side of a kitchen knife. (A ruler will do if it is thinner than the coin.)

Do this trick in the garden using plastic picnic cups or unbreakable camping mugs and plates. Lay the table, put water in the cups, then see if you can whip the cloth away without spilling anything.

SNATCH THE CLOTH AWAY WITH A HARD LEVEL PULL.

The scientific detective
If you have one raw egg and one hard-boiled egg, you can use some simple science to tell which is which. Turn this into a game and challenge your friends to find the raw egg (*not* by dropping the eggs). Spin the eggs on a plate, then touch each one quickly with a finger but let go again at once. One egg will stop. The other will keep on spinning. That one is the raw egg. Can you work out why?

Inertia keeps the liquid inside the raw egg swirling round, and that starts the egg turning again.

Balancing

With a piece of thread, a pin and a weight you can find the balance point of any flat cut-out shape. Hang the card and the weighted thread from the pin like this. Gravity will pull on the weight and make the string point straight down. Draw a line very carefully where the thread crosses the card. Hang the shape from another place on the card and draw a second line. The cut-out figure should balance exactly where the lines cross.

You could stick a picture on to stiff card and cut it out.

FIRST LINE

SECOND LINE

Scientists call this the 'centre of gravity' of the shape.

How far can it tilt?

Solid objects have a centre of gravity too. The lower down it is, the harder it is to tip the object over. That is why things like table lamps have a heavy base. See how far you can tilt an empty match box before it falls. Then try again with a rubber in the box, and finally with a heavy weight inside. Try a bolt with several nuts on it.

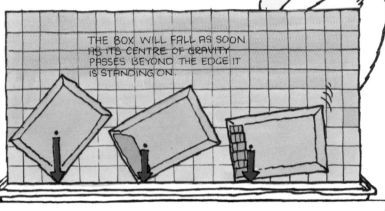

THE BOX WILL FALL AS SOON AS ITS CENTRE OF GRAVITY PASSES BEYOND THE EDGE IT IS STANDING ON.

Testing for safety

All the heavy parts of the bus are close to the ground so there is no danger of it tipping over.

The top deck is made from very light materials.

Engine, gearbox and other heavy parts are all low down.

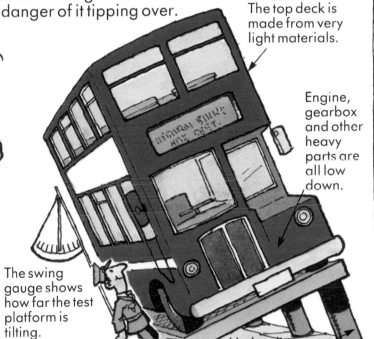

The swing gauge shows how far the test platform is tilting.

Test platform

Hydraulic rams (see pages 26-27)

An 'impossible' balancing act

You can even make 'impossible' things balance if you cheat and change the centre of gravity. This model tightrope walker could never stand on the string without help. His centre of gravity is above the string and he would topple off. But if you hang a weight from his arms, that lowers the centre of gravity of the whole toy. Now it is below the tightrope and he is quite safe.

USE A SMALL CORK FOR THE HEAD

PIN THE HEAD TO THE BOX

BENT CARD GLUED TO THE BOX

TAPE

STRAW

TAPE

THIN STRING

SPLIT THE STRAW AND GLUE TO PAPER FEET

STRAW

LUMP OF PLASTICINE

Adding the plasticine brings the centre of gravity down here. The model's weight is now helping him stay on the string.

IF YOU SWING THE WEIGHT GENTLY, THE TIGHTROPE WALKER WILL WALK ALONG THE STRING

Magnifying muscles

Most simple machines, like levers and wedges and pulleys, work on the same idea. A small amount of 'effort' (the work you do) moves over quite a large distance. The machine then turns this into a bigger force moving only a short distance. This way, a machine can make a difficult or heavy job much easier.

Many of these simple machines have been used for thousands of years, but for most of that time they had to be worked by human muscles alone. Then water and wind power (pages 22-23) were harnessed to machines, and later still (in the last 300 years) steam engines, petrol engines and electric motors were invented.

More than 2,000 years ago the great Greek scientist Archimedes said, 'Give me somewhere to stand, and I will move the earth.'

What he said was quite true—at least in theory. But he would have needed a lever millions of kilometres long, *and* somewhere to rest the lever, *and* somewhere to stand way out in space!

Different levers for different jobs

Levers can be made to do different jobs depending on where you put the effort (that is, the work *you* do), the fulcrum (where the lever rocks or turns), and the load (the thing you want to move).

The longer your lever or crowbar is, the easier it will be to lift the rock.

Here the effort and the load are both at the same side of the fulcrum—but the lifting effort still has the longest lever.

This kind of lever magnifies movement. A small movement at the bottom of the rod makes the tip move a long way.

The chemist's weighing machine

This weighing machine works like the coin-and-ruler experiment on the opposite page. Your weight pulls on the short arm of a see-saw lever and this is balanced by a smaller weight working a much longer lever.

The counterweight balances the long arm at the other side so that the machine always starts off level.

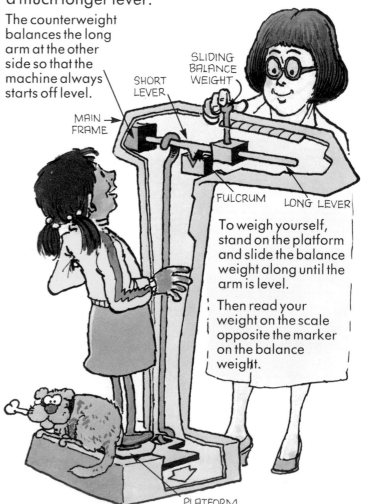

To weigh yourself, stand on the platform and slide the balance weight along until the arm is level.

Then read your weight on the scale opposite the marker on the balance weight.

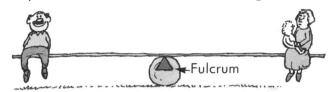

How levers work

Put two coins on each end of a 20cm ruler and balance it across a pencil. Now try adding two more coins at one end. The ruler will still balance if you place these coins 5cm away from the pencil. This is because each side of the ruler is working as a lever, and two coins pressing on a 10cm lever give as much force as four coins pressing on a 5cm lever.

You can experiment with levers using a plank. Here, the balance point (called the fulcrum) is at the centre and the plank is level, so Dad must be as heavy as Mum and Freddie added together.

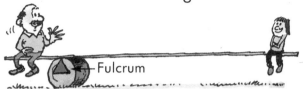

This time Jenny has moved the fulcrum to give herself a very long lever. It has multiplied her weight so much that she can lift Dad right off the ground. She has made a lifting machine.

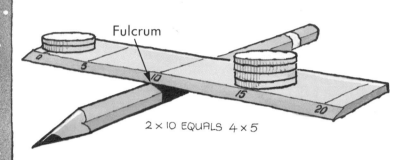

2 × 10 EQUALS 4 × 5

Levers that write letters

Can you match any of the typewriter levers with the ones in the side panel?

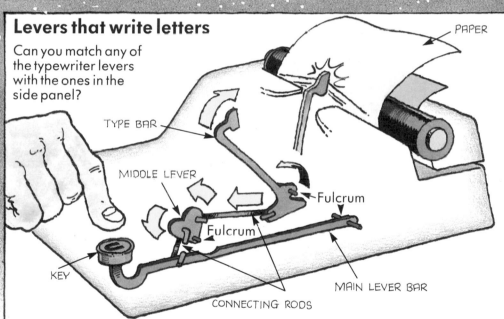

PAPER

TYPE BAR

MIDDLE LEVER

Fulcrum

Fulcrum

KEY

CONNECTING RODS

MAIN LEVER BAR

The mechanical typewriter is worked almost entirely by levers. When you strike a key, the main lever bar moves down and a connecting rod pulls the next lever. This gives a sharp pull to the bottom end of the final lever – the type bar – and this flies over and prints a letter on the page.

Launch-pad levers

This daring circus act is using a see-saw type of lever to send one member of the team flying high into the air. Why do you think the young boy was chosen for this trick? Would he go as high if just one adult jumped on the launching pad?

Fulcrum

Levers for lazybones

'Lazy-tongs' are simply chains of levers linked together. You could make some from the pieces of a construction kit, or simply from scrap wood.

Fulcrum

A couple of old teaspoons make handy 'grabbers'.

Slopes and screws

One of the simplest ways of moving a heavy weight is to drag it up a slope instead of trying to lift it straight up. The ancient Egyptians used this method when they built the great pyramids more than 4,500 years ago.

Huge numbers of workers were needed to drag the stones up the earth slope.

Each of the blocks in the Great Pyramid weighed about 2 tons.

The earth ramp had to be built higher for each layer of stones.

Men at the back used levers to push the heavy stones forward.

Wooden rollers were probably used to help move the block along.

Experiments with slopes

For these experiments you will need a force measurer. Page 5 tells you how to make one quite easily. Use your force measurer to see how much pull is needed to lift a toy lorry straight up from the floor.

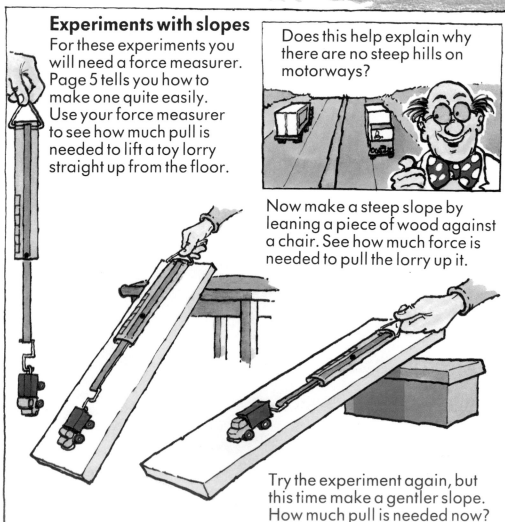

Does this help explain why there are no steep hills on motorways?

Now make a steep slope by leaning a piece of wood against a chair. See how much force is needed to pull the lorry up it.

Try the experiment again, but this time make a gentler slope. How much pull is needed now?

Using a wedge

A wedge works like two slopes stuck back to back. But instead of moving the load up the slope, you force the slope past the load. Here, the load is the log you want to split.

A blow with a hammer drives the wedge part way in. The wedge turns this into a much bigger force, pushing sideways to open up the split.

Rolling up a slope

If you walk up a hill on a spiral path it is much easier than going straight up. A screw works on the same idea. It is simply a long slope that has been 'rolled up' so it takes up less space. The more turns a screw has, the longer its 'path' is and the less effort it takes to move a load along it.

One turn of a piano stool with a gentle screw thread does not raise the seat far, but is easy to do.

A steep thread on the lifting screw raises the seat much more but it takes a lot more effort.

You can check the 'rolled up slope' idea like this. Cut out a paper slope and wind it on to a pencil. Then follow the edge of the paper with your finger.

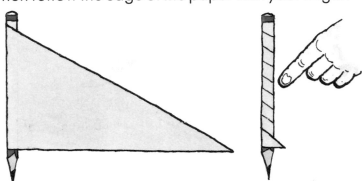

Screws with gently sloping threads move along slowly and take longer to do up, but they do not need as much effort as steep screw threads.

Machines that use screws

You can use a vice to hold things steady as you work, or to squeeze a joint tightly while the glue is drying. When you turn the handle, the screw is pulled through the threaded hole in the fixed part of the vice and the movable jaw closes.

The wood-drilling bit uses two kinds of screws. A small 'leader' screw pulls the drill into the wood so the cutters can do their job. Then the wood chips slide up the spiral screw so they do not clog up the hole.

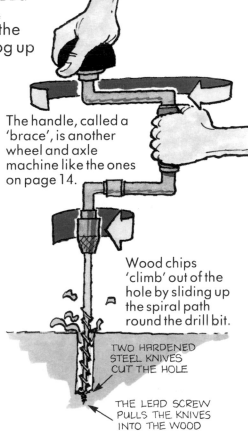

The handle, called a 'brace', is another wheel and axle machine like the ones on page 14.

Wood chips 'climb' out of the hole by sliding up the spiral path round the drill bit.

TWO HARDENED STEEL KNIVES CUT THE HOLE

THE LEAD SCREW PULLS THE KNIVES INTO THE WOOD

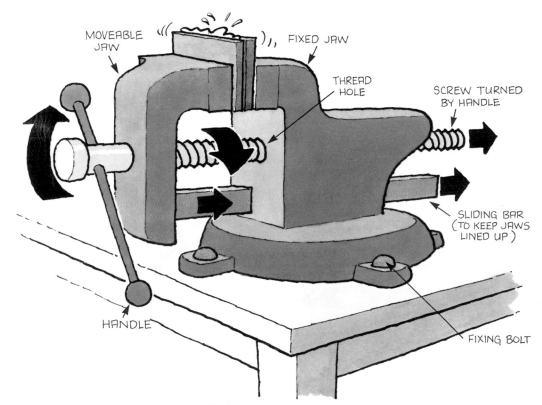

MOVEABLE JAW

FIXED JAW

THREAD HOLE

SCREW TURNED BY HANDLE

SLIDING BAR (TO KEEP JAWS LINED UP)

HANDLE

FIXING BOLT

Wheels, axles and pulleys

The wheel and axle idea has been used in machines for thousands of years. It works like a non-stop lever and, like an ordinary lever, it can turn a small force on the winding handle into a much more powerful force on the axle. This kind of machine is used in old-fashioned wells and in ships' capstans, but you can also see it in action turning a car steering wheel or working the pedals of a bicycle.

Drawing water from an old-fashioned well.

A neat safety device

The ratchet is a very useful little gadget. It allows the axle to turn one way, but when you stop winding the peg catches on the teeth and stops the axle spinning backwards.

Raising the anchor with a capstan turned by long levers.

The power of the pulley

In a pulley system, the force of the pull is spread right through the rope, so the more strands there are holding the weight up, the more the load is shared out.

Two pulleys will double your lifting power because the weight is being shared between two strands of rope.

Four pulleys, arranged like this, will give you four times as much lifting power.

Here is a good trick. The 2 kilogramme counterweight is helping you, so you only have to lift half the weight yourself.

One pulley is not much help. It only alters the direction of pull.

14

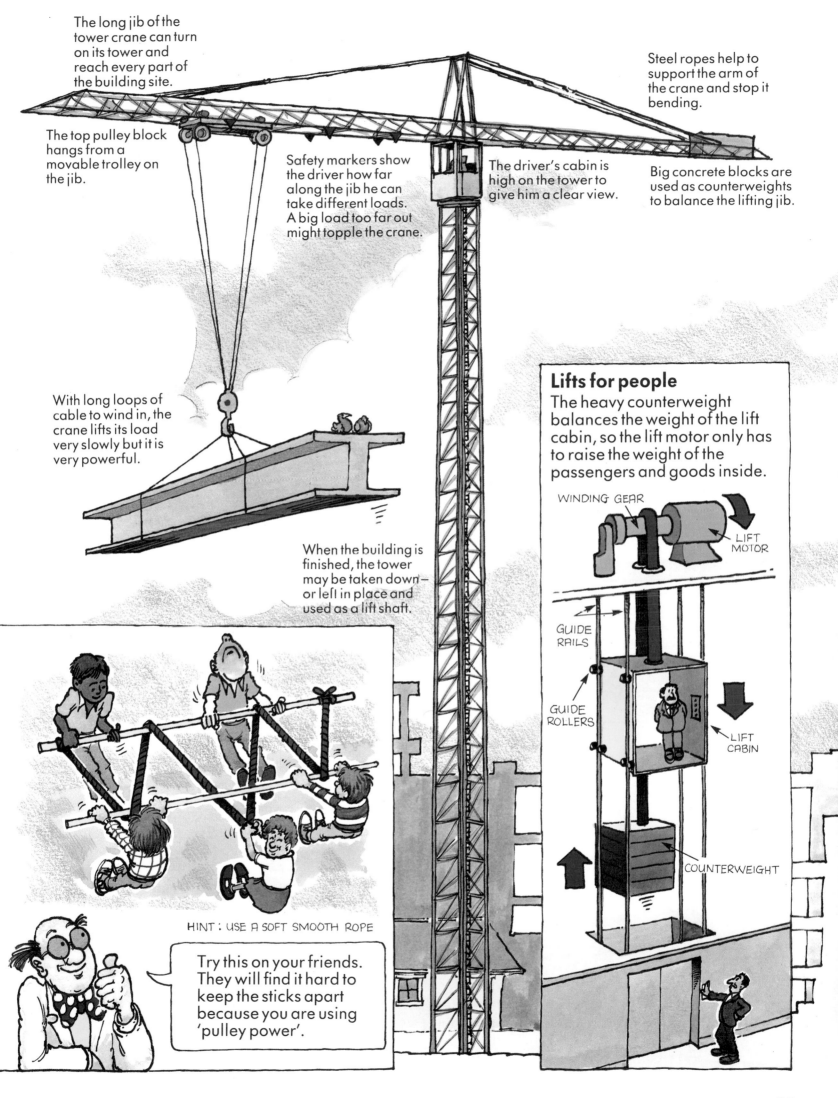

The long jib of the tower crane can turn on its tower and reach every part of the building site.

Steel ropes help to support the arm of the crane and stop it bending.

The top pulley block hangs from a movable trolley on the jib.

Safety markers show the driver how far along the jib he can take different loads. A big load too far out might topple the crane.

The driver's cabin is high on the tower to give him a clear view.

Big concrete blocks are used as counterweights to balance the lifting jib.

With long loops of cable to wind in, the crane lifts its load very slowly but it is very powerful.

When the building is finished, the tower may be taken down— or left in place and used as a lift shaft.

Lifts for people
The heavy counterweight balances the weight of the lift cabin, so the lift motor only has to raise the weight of the passengers and goods inside.

WINDING GEAR

LIFT MOTOR

GUIDE RAILS

GUIDE ROLLERS

LIFT CABIN

COUNTERWEIGHT

HINT : USE A SOFT SMOOTH ROPE

Try this on your friends. They will find it hard to keep the sticks apart because you are using 'pulley power'.

Sticking and slipping

What happens when you rub your hands together very quickly? They get warm. The force that causes this is called friction. It is a force that tries to stop things sliding past each other. Sometimes friction is very useful. Without it our feet would just slip when we tried to walk. It was probably the first way man found of making fire. And it is what makes car and bicycle brakes work. But there are also times when friction is a great nuisance. Engineers try to get rid of it in their machines because it makes moving parts get hot, and wears them out, and also wastes energy.

Spinning the stick very fast eventually makes the tinder (dry grass) start to smoulder.

The soldier sliding down a rope controls his speed by the friction between the rope and his clothing. But please don't try to copy him. It takes special training to do this safely.

Braking power

A bicycle brake uses the friction between a hard rubber pad and the metal rim of the wheel. When you squeeze the brake lever, another set of levers presses the pads against the rim and slows the wheel down. Feel the rim after braking hard; it will be warm.

Pincer levers

Brake pads

Unsticking sticky drawers

If you rub a soft lead pencil (such as HB or 2B) on a piece of paper and then rub your finger over the black mark, you will find that it is very slippery. You can use this tip to make a sticking drawer slide in and out smoothly.

Experimenting with friction forces

Use your force measurer to see how much pull it takes just to start a block of wood sliding along a board. Test again, first with some smooth shiny paper under the bottom of the block, then with sandpaper. Smooth surfaces slide easily, rough ones cause a lot of friction. You can also try rubbing the block with a candle or wax crayon, or put some oil on the board. What happens then?

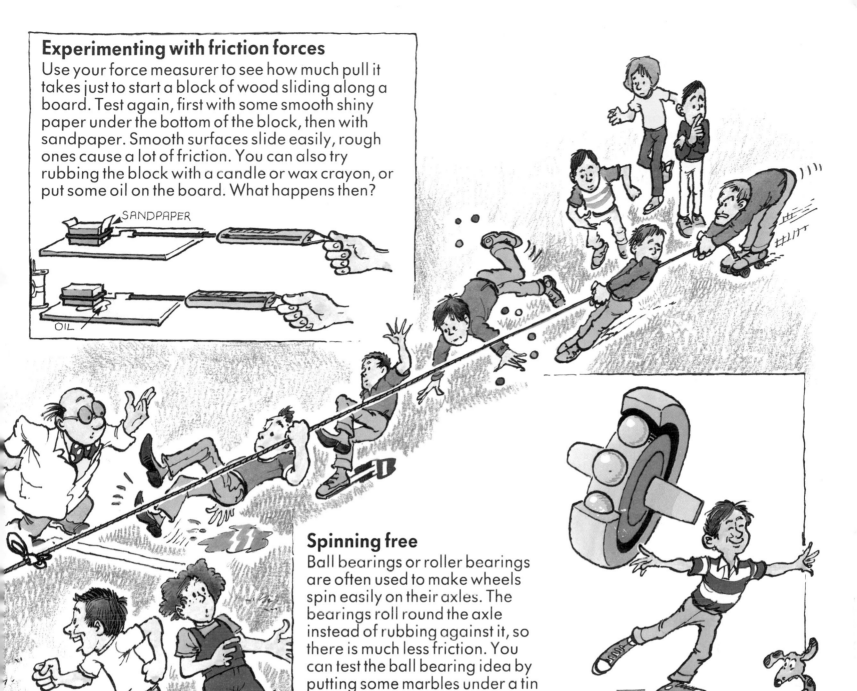

Spinning free

Ball bearings or roller bearings are often used to make wheels spin easily on their axles. The bearings roll round the axle instead of rubbing against it, so there is much less friction. You can test the ball bearing idea by putting some marbles under a tin lid and rolling it across the floor.

Floating without friction

The hovercraft lifts itself clear of the ground on a cushion of air, so it has very little trouble with friction. Huge fans suck air in above deck and blow it out underneath the hovercraft where it is trapped by a rubber skirt. A big hovercraft like the SRN4 can carry 254 passengers and 30 cars.

A yoghurt pot and a polystyrene food tray from a supermarket are all you need to make your own hovercraft.

The propellers drive the hovercraft forward, and can swivel on their mounts to steer left or right.

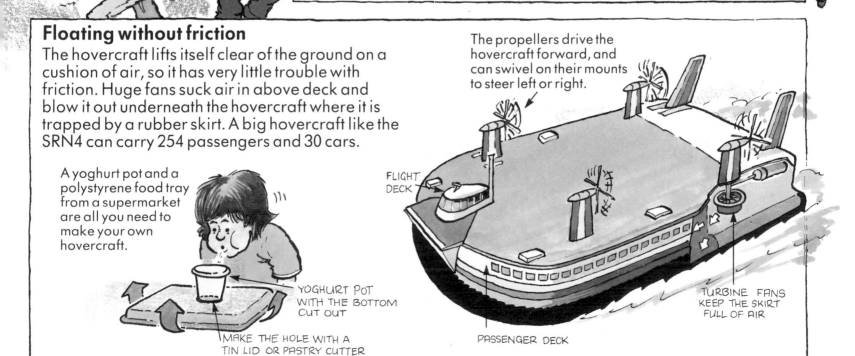

YOGHURT POT WITH THE BOTTOM CUT OUT

MAKE THE HOLE WITH A TIN LID OR PASTRY CUTTER

FLIGHT DECK

PASSENGER DECK

TURBINE FANS KEEP THE SKIRT FULL OF AIR

Whirling around

Whenever you ride on a playground roundabout you can feel a force pressing you outwards. The faster you whirl round, the stronger the force becomes and the tighter you have to hold on. This outward force works on anything that is whirling around – and it can be very useful. It can be used to control machines, or to spin clothes dry, or even to provide artificial gravity for scientists working in space stations. Man-made satellites stay in orbit because the outward force caused by their whirling movement just balances the inward pull of Earth's gravity. As soon as they slow down, they fall back to Earth. You can show how this works with a simple experiment.

Satellites in orbit

Thread a length of fishing line or thin string through the case of an old ball-point pen. Then tie a paper clip very firmly to each end. Press a ball of plasticene weighing about 10g round one paper clip, and a larger ball weighing about 50g round the other paper clip.

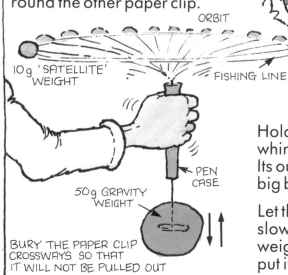

10g 'SATELLITE' WEIGHT

ORBIT

FISHING LINE

PEN CASE

50g GRAVITY WEIGHT

BURY THE PAPER CLIP CROSSWAYS SO THAT IT WILL NOT BE PULLED OUT

Why doesn't the water fall out of the bucket?

Hold the pen-case upright and whirl the small 'satellite' round. Its outward pull will raise the big ball even though it is heavier.

Let the satellite slow down. As it slows, its pull gets less and the weight of the larger ball will put it back into a small orbit.

Science at the fairground

Fairground rides and motorcycle stuntmen use the outward force of whirling objects to do things that look impossible.

The outward force presses the people against the wall of the 'Roundup' ride. They do not even have to hold on.

Roundup

The faster the roundabout turns, the higher the chairs will fly. (Remember the experiment on page 6?)

Whirling the water away

Automatic washing machines use the whirling force. At the end of the wash, most of the water is pumped out of the machine. Then the motor starts the drum spinning very fast. The soggy clothes are pressed hard against the inside of the drum – just like the people on the fairground 'Roundup'. The clothes can go no farther, but the water can. It gets spun out through the hundreds of holes in the surface of the drum.

The same force holds the 'Death Spiral' car on its loop-the-loop track, even when it is upside down.

The 'Wall of Death' rider can stay on the wall as long as he is going very fast.

Making gravity in space

Space stations of the future will spin like the sails of a windmill. The middle section turns slowly, so supply ships can dock there, but the living areas and workshops at the ends of the arms are moving quite fast.

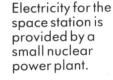

Spinning movement

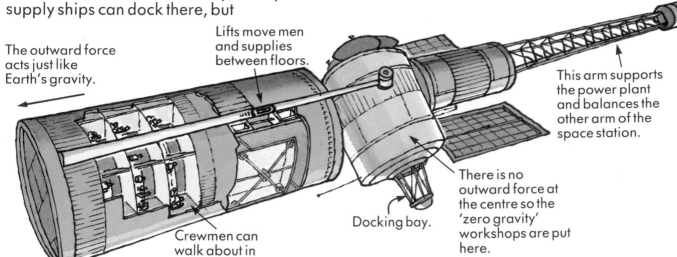

The outward force acts just like Earth's gravity.

Lifts move men and supplies between floors.

This arm supports the power plant and balances the other arm of the space station.

Electricity for the space station is provided by a small nuclear power plant.

There is no outward force at the centre so the 'zero gravity' workshops are put here.

Docking bay.

Crewmen can walk about in artificial gravity.

Make a model space station

For the power unit, make a small hole in the base of a washing-up liquid bottle. Thread a thick rubber band through it. Anchor the band with a matchstick taped to the bottom of the bottle. Make a hook at the end of a piece of strong wire and catch hold of the band through the top of the bottle.

1

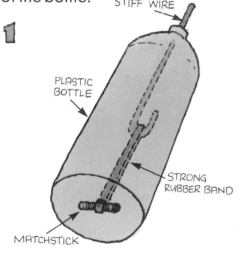

STIFF WIRE

PLASTIC BOTTLE

STRONG RUBBER BAND

MATCHSTICK

2

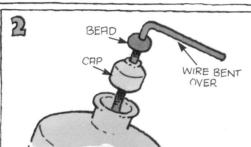

BEAD

CAP

WIRE BENT OVER

Cut the stopper off the bottle top and thread the top on to the wire. Add a small bead, then bend the wire over to one side.

3

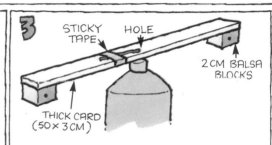

STICKY TAPE   HOLE

2 CM BALSA BLOCKS

THICK CARD (50 × 3 CM)

Make the arm from a piece of thick card, 50cm × 3cm, and glue a small balsa block to each end. Fix the arm to the wire with tape.

4

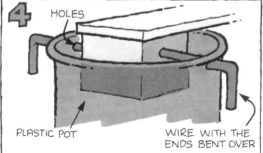

HOLES

PLASTIC POT

WIRE WITH THE ENDS BENT OVER

Drill a small hole through each block. Make holes in two clear plastic food pots, then use stiff wire to hang them on the arms.

5

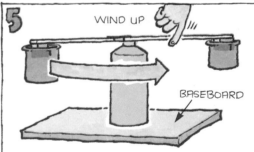

WIND UP

BASEBOARD

Glue the space station to a flat board to keep it steady. Then wind up the rubber band motor (about 50 turns) for a test spin.

6

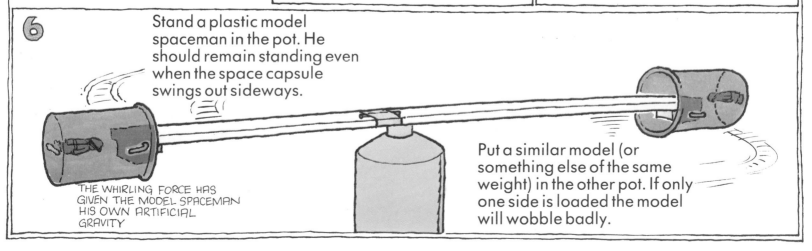

Stand a plastic model spaceman in the pot. He should remain standing even when the space capsule swings out sideways.

THE WHIRLING FORCE HAS GIVEN THE MODEL SPACEMAN HIS OWN ARTIFICIAL GRAVITY

Put a similar model (or something else of the same weight) in the other pot. If only one side is loaded the model will wobble badly.

19

Changing speed and direction

In any big complicated machine, all sorts of different moving parts will be in action at the same time. Some will be moving very quickly and others quite slowly. Some may be spinning round and round while others are bobbing up and down. One bit might be turning in one direction while the part next to it is turning the opposite way.

It would be very wasteful to have a separate motor driving each part, so large numbers of gears, belts, drive chains and connecting rods are used to take the power of the motor to different parts of the machine, and to alter its speed and direction once it gets there. Try spotting speed and direction changes in other machines in this book – like the typewriter (page 11), the lift (page 15), the windmill (page 22) and the steam engine (page 28).

Experimenting with home-made gears

Use the patterns on page 2 to make a set of gears like the ones below. For the experiments, fix your gears to a flat piece of wood with drawing pins through the centre. The teeth should interlock, but not tightly. Mark one tooth on each gear so you can follow it.

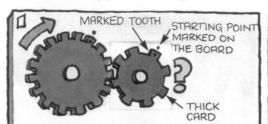
MARKED TOOTH — STARTING POINT MARKED ON THE BOARD — THICK CARD

Turn the large blue gear through one complete turn. How many turns does the red gear make? And which way does it turn?

This time turn the small red gear through one complete turn. Watch what happens to the blue gear.

Now try it with three gears, two large ones and one small one. Make a full turn with the left-hand gear. What happens to the other two?

What controls the speed of the last gear in each row? (Hint: try counting teeth.)

Gears that tell the time

The energy stored in the main spring is released a little at a time by the escape wheel and lever. This energy is fed to the clock hands by a set of gears.

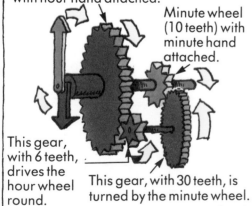

Hour wheel (24 teeth) with hour hand attached.

Minute wheel (10 teeth) with minute hand attached.

This gear, with 6 teeth, drives the hour wheel round.

This gear, with 30 teeth, is turned by the minute wheel.

The number of teeth on each gear wheel is carefully worked out so that the minute hand goes round 12 times in the same time it takes the hour hand to go round once.

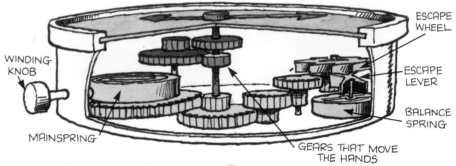
WINDING KNOB — MAINSPRING — ESCAPE WHEEL — ESCAPE LEVER — BALANCE SPRING — GEARS THAT MOVE THE HANDS

The six o'clock puzzle

Suppose we start with the hands like this, at six o'clock. We know how many teeth each wheel has, and we know that the two drive gears are fixed together, so if one makes a full turn, so does the other. Can you work out what time the clock will show when the drive gears have made one full turn?

It will show nine o'clock. The minute wheel will have made three turns, and the hour wheel will have made a quarter turn.

DRIVE GEARS

Driving, turning, bobbing and rocking

The car engine is a marvellous example of lots of moving parts all working together. Follow the action on the drawing. Petrol explodes in the cylinder and drives the piston down. The connecting rod turns the crankshaft and a toothed wheel at the far end moves a chain. This turns another wheel on the camshaft, and each time the pear-shaped cam comes round it lifts the push-rod. Finally the top of the push-rod works a rocking lever and this opens and shuts the valve to let in the next squirt of petrol.

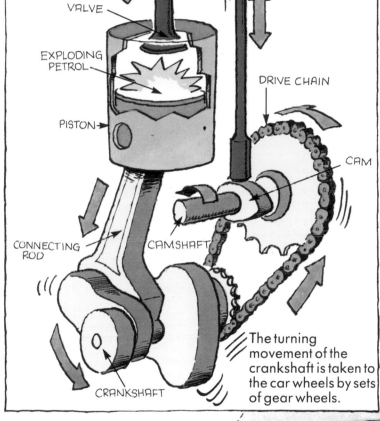

ROCKER
SPRING
FULCRUM
PUSH ROD
VALVE
EXPLODING PETROL
PISTON
DRIVE CHAIN
CAM
CONNECTING ROD
CAMSHAFT
CRANKSHAFT

The turning movement of the crankshaft is taken to the car wheels by sets of gear wheels.

The high-speed egg-whisk

A simple egg-whisk uses two gears to change the fairly slow winding action of the handle into a much faster spinning movement of the whisk. And because the teeth are on the side of the big gear, not on the edge, the machine changes the direction of the movement at the same time.

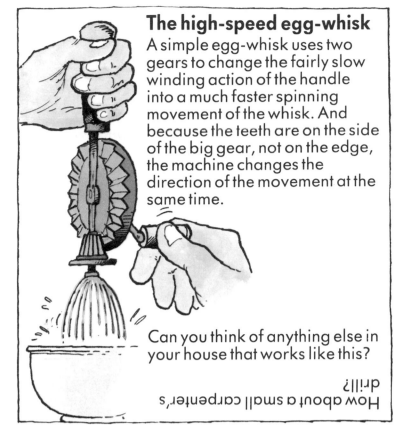

Can you think of anything else in your house that works like this?

How about a small carpenter's drill?

Wheels and gears in action

This bike has lots of different mechanical parts. By now you will know how most of them work.

Levers work the brakes.

Friction works the brakes here.

Bearings make the wheels spin smoothly.

A wheel and axle machine provides the power.

The chain drives the back wheel.

Friction here makes the bike go forward.

Power from nature

Watermills have been used as a source of power for more than 2,000 years. At first they were used to power corn mills, but later they drove blacksmiths' forges, water pumps and weaving and spinning machines. They were easy to build, hardly ever broke down and cost nothing to run. Windmills have not been around for quite so long, but they too have been used all over the world for more than 1,000 years.

Nowadays, most of our machines are powered by electricity, made by power stations burning coal or expensive oil. Other machines, like cars and aeroplanes, burn petrol, diesel or aviation fuel, also made from oil. So engineers have started to look again at new ways of using cheap natural power – from the wind, the rivers, and even the ocean tides.

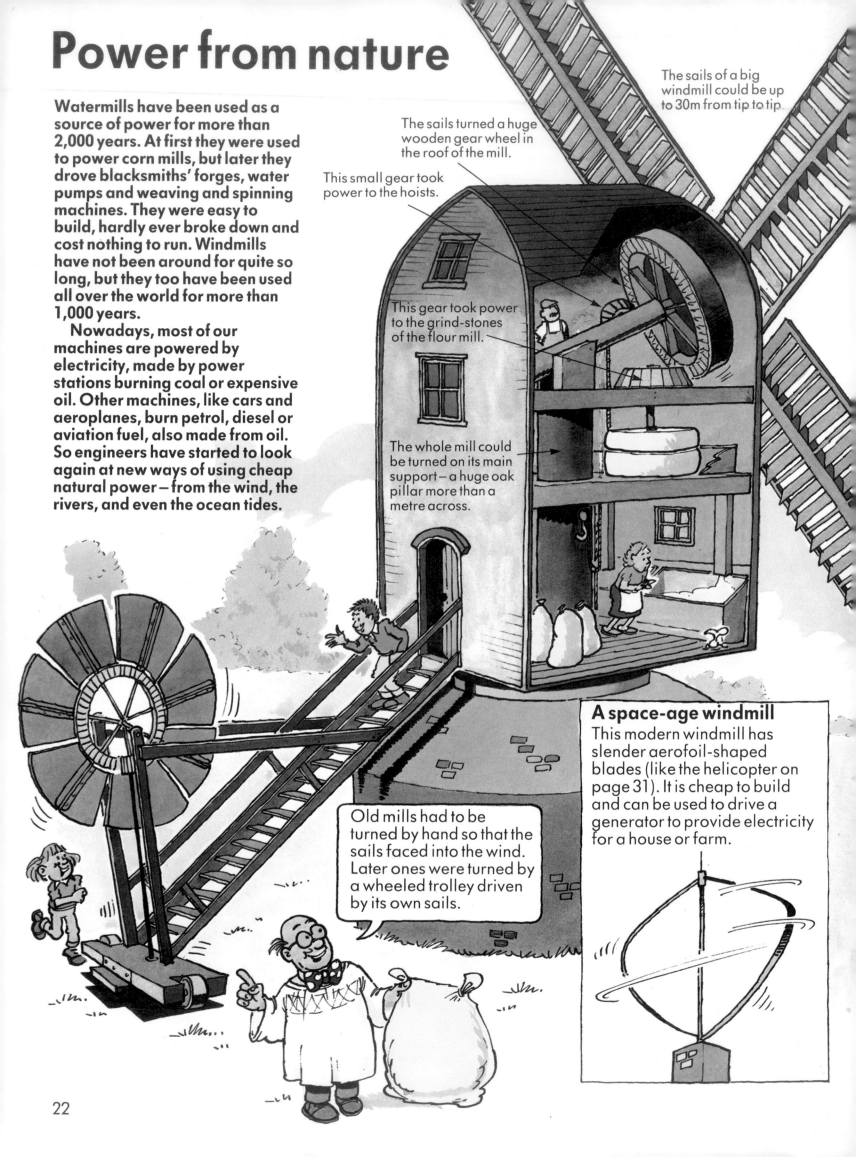

The sails of a big windmill could be up to 30m from tip to tip

The sails turned a huge wooden gear wheel in the roof of the mill.

This small gear took power to the hoists.

This gear took power to the grind-stones of the flour mill.

The whole mill could be turned on its main support – a huge oak pillar more than a metre across.

Old mills had to be turned by hand so that the sails faced into the wind. Later ones were turned by a wheeled trolley driven by its own sails.

A space-age windmill
This modern windmill has slender aerofoil-shaped blades (like the helicopter on page 31). It is cheap to build and can be used to drive a generator to provide electricity for a house or farm.

A simple spinner

You can make a windmill quite easily from a square of stiff paper, a long pin, a bead and a stick. Draw lines from corner to corner, then cut half-way from the corner to the middle.

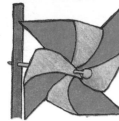

Bend each of the marked corners into the centre and push the pin through them. Slip a bead on to the pin then push it into the stick. See which way it spins. What could you do to make it spin the other way?

Can you believe your eyes?

Draw a robber on one side of a piece of card, and the prison bars on the other. Tape two long pins to the card like this, then blow the card to spin the robber straight into jail.

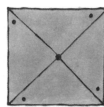

Water power at work

Next time you see a waterwheel see if you can work out how it was turned. Undershot wheels got all their power from the mill stream pushing against the flat blades as it rushed underneath the wheel. Overshot wheels were turned partly by the force of the rushing water and partly by the weight of the water caught in the scoop-shaped blades. They made much better use of the power of the mill stream.

Make your own water turbine

This kind of waterwheel is called a Pelton wheel. It uses a jet of water aimed at the spoon-shaped turbine blades. Can you guess what happens to the speed of the wheel as the bottle empties?

LARGE PLASTIC BOTTLE

PLASTIC PICNIC TEASPOONS

DARNING NEEDLE

LARGE CORK

MAKE THE SUPPORTS FROM TWO FORKS FIRMLY TIED TO HEAVY FOOD TINS

PLASTICINE

PLASTIC DRINKING STRAW

AIM THE WATER JET AT THE MIDDLE OF THE SPOON

Power from the sea

This tidal power station forms a dam across the mouth of a river on the coast of France. Its special turbines can spin in either direction, so electricity can be generated when the rising tide flows in from the sea through the turbine tunnels, and then again when the water trapped behind the dam is allowed to flood back out as the tide falls.

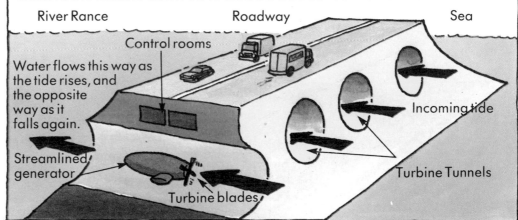

River Rance

Roadway

Sea

Control rooms

Water flows this way as the tide rises, and the opposite way as it falls again.

Streamlined generator

Turbine blades

Incoming tide

Turbine Tunnels

Putting on the pressure

It is very easy to think that air has no weight at all, but it has. The atmosphere presses down and around us, just as the water in the ocean presses on the hull of a submarine. Fortunately, our bodies are specially designed for life at the bottom of this 'ocean of air' and we do not even notice that more than a kilogramme of air is pressing on every square centimetre of our skin. There are plenty of good experiments to show that air pressure is all around us.

AIR PRESSURE

INERTIA

Breaking the rule
Place a thin old wooden ruler on the table with about 8cm sticking over the edge. Then lay several sheets of newspaper over the ruler and smooth them out flat. Bring your fist down hard on the end of the ruler, and see what happens.

Did the newspaper fly up in the air as you might expect? If it didn't, what do you think held it down?

The invisible bottle-squasher
Very carefully pour some hot water into a plastic drinks bottle. Wait a few seconds for the steam to rise, then screw the top on tightly. Can you guess what will happen as the bottle cools down?

Rising steam pushes some of the air out.

The steam cools and turns back to water, leaving an empty space.

Now there is nothing to stop the outside air pressure squashing the bottle inwards.

No air can get in

Upside-down magic
Fill a tumbler with water, right to the brim, then lay a post-card across the top. Hold it in place and carefully turn the glass upside down. Take away the hand holding the card. Did your feet get wet?

1 BRIMFULL

2

3

4

WHAT IS HOLDING THE CARD IN PLACE?

Using air as a spring
If you squash air, or any other gas, into a smaller space, it pushes back. It is trying to spread out again and fill the space it used to have before you 'compressed' it. This pushing back is very useful. It makes the gas behave like a spring. If you block the end of a cycle pump with your finger, then push the handle in hard, you will feel the springiness of the compressed air inside the pump.

The 'hobby-horse' had solid wooden wheels and was a real bone-shaker.

Pulling the piston out

Air leak past the washer here.

Air gets in here.

And fills the space here.

Pushing the piston in

This end is blocked.

Air cannot get back this way.

The piston handle feels springy.

The washer spreads out.

The air in here is compressed.

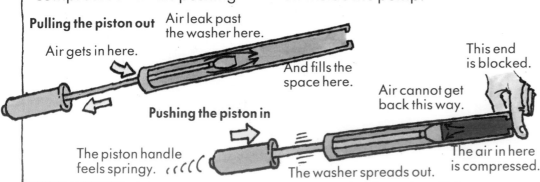

Modern bicycles have air-filled tyres that cushion the shocks.

How high can you go?

When you drink through a straw, all you really do is suck some of the air out of the straw. This makes the pressure inside the straw less than the pressure outside. It is the air pressing on the lemonade in the glass that pushes the drink up the straw to balance the pressure again.

The longest straw you could ever use would reach about 10 metres above the glass. That is as high as the air pressure could push your drink.

Air-pressure clues for the weatherman

When the TV weatherman makes his forecast he often talks about the 'Highs' and 'Lows' on his chart. These are areas where the air pressure is higher or lower than normal, and they are good clues to the sort of weather we can expect. High pressure usually brings fine settled weather, but low pressure brings bad weather with blustery winds and rain.

FAIR
CHANGE
STORM

THE TOP OF THE BOX CAN MOVE UP AND DOWN

THIS SIDE OF THE BOX IS FIXED TO THE CASE

THE SPRING STOPS THE BOX BEING SQUASHED FLAT

LEVERS THAT MOVE THE POINTER

Weather scientists (meteorologists) measure the air pressure with a barometer. Inside it is a metal box with nearly all the air taken out. High air pressure pushes the top of the box inwards, and a system of levers makes the pointer move round the dial. When the air pressure drops, the lid springs out again and the pointer moves the other way, warning of bad weather.

Big soft 'balloon' tyres can cope with very rough ground.

'Space-hopper' toys use the springiness of air compressed inside a strong rubber ball.

Some kinds of car shock absorbers work just like the cycle pump experiment. They have a piston inside that squashes a gas when the wheel hits a bump.

Heavy tankers and lorries have lots of wheels to spread their weight out.

Pumping and lifting

One of the big differences between gases and liquids is that liquids cannot be squashed. If you try the bicycle pump experiment on page 24, but fill the pump with water rather than air, you will not be able to compress the water at all. It will push back on the piston just as hard as you press in on the handle. This is a clue to another important group of machines. They are called hydraulic machines and they use liquids, usually a type of oil, to push pistons backwards and forwards inside cylinders. By using different sizes of cylinders the force can be magnified many times – to operate big heavy machines.

Can water be compressed?

Suck some water into the pump.

Block the end of the cylinder and try to compress the water inside.

Keep pushing, and see what happens when you take your finger away from the hole.

You can feel the difference between gases and liquids during fun-time at the pool.

AIR IS SPRINGY

WATER ISN'T

Water-power

MAKE A SMALL GAP HERE SO THE AIR IN THE BOTTLE CAN GET OUT

Surprise your friends with this experiment. It proves the lifting power of water.

Fix a length of plastic tube or old garden hose into the neck of a hot-water bottle. (You may need a little help to get a watertight joint.) Then pile some heavy books on the bottle and carefully pour some water down the tube. You might expect the weight of the books to keep the bottle squashed flat, but to everyone's amazement it will fill with water and lift the books off the floor.

Lifting, pushing and squeezing with liquids

The great thing about trying to squash a liquid is that it pushes back with the same force in all directions. It makes no difference if the liquid is in a pipe with lots of bends, or in a square tank, or in a floppy bag like a hot-water bottle. The pressure spreads out evenly so that every square centimetre of the container has the same force pressing on it. This means that liquids can be used a bit like levers, to turn small forces into big ones. If the liquid is put inside two different-sized cylinders, joined by a pipe, a small force on the small piston will produce a much bigger force on the big piston.

1 KG PUSH

10 CM

This piston only moves a small distance, but its surface is ten times bigger than the other piston so it gives ten times as much push.

10 KG PUSH

10 SQ CM PISTON

OIL-FILLED PIPE

100 SQ CM PISTON

1CM

The books were raised because the water in the tube acted like the small piston, and the bottle pushed upwards like the big one.

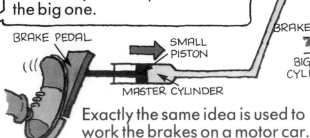

BRAKE PEDAL

SMALL PISTON

MASTER CYLINDER

BRAKE PIPE

BRAKE PADS

BIG BRAKE CYLINDER

SPINNING BRAKE DISC

Exactly the same idea is used to work the brakes on a motor car.

The village pump

The kind of pump you sometimes see on a village green is called a lift pump. A lever handle moves the piston inside the cylinder and simple valves, often made of flaps of leather, control the flow of water. Each time the handle is moved, one valve opens and the other closes. Water gushes from the spout each time the piston moves upwards. It is a bit like scooping up water with your hands.

The fireman's pump

This type is called a force pump. It squirts the water out much harder than a lift pump can. It has two valves as well, but they are both below the piston. The up-stroke of the piston fills the cylinder with water, then the downstroke forces it out through the pipe, like squirting water from between your hands. Firemen used pumps like this before powerful motor-driven pumps were invented.

The heavy brigade

If two-way valves are added to hydraulic cylinders, the pistons can be made to push in either direction (just like the steam-engine pistons on page 28). That is how the powerful rams on a bulldozer can gently lift and lower the huge steel blade. See how many hydraulics you can find in this illustration.

The age of steam

Two hundred years ago, the world was a much quieter place. There were no engines, or cars, or big industrial cities. Machines were powered by people, or by windmills or waterwheels. But everything changed when the steam engine was invented. It could be big or small. It could be powered by burning coal or wood. And most important of all it provided power wherever power was needed. Very soon, more people were living in cities than in the country. Huge factories were built to spin cotton and make cloth, and forge iron for bridges, ships and railways.

The early steam engine shown here used a coal-fired boiler to make steam. This was piped to the main cylinder where it forced a piston up and down. The piston was connected to a big wooden beam that rocked back and forth, turning the huge iron flywheel.

Any idea what this is? (Have a look at the opposite page.)

BEAM
CYLINDER
STEAM
GOVERNOR
CONNECTING ROD
FLYWHEEL
FURNACE

The spinning flywheel could be used to drive other machines.

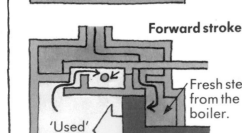

Steam inlet
Forward stroke
Steam outlet pipe
Sliding valve
Piston rod

Return stroke
Used steam left from the forward stroke.

Forward stroke
Fresh steam from the boiler.
'Used' steam

Getting the power to the wheels

The huge driving wheels of a steam locomotive are turned by connecting rods pushed backwards and forwards by pistons in the cylinders. A sliding valve lets steam in at one side of the piston to push it one way, then lets steam in at the other side to push it back again.

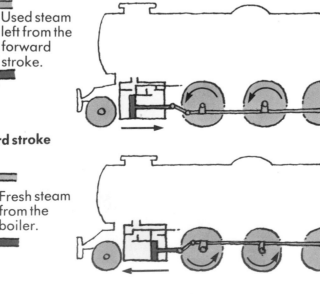

Engines for every job

Steam engines came in all shapes and sizes, from the small shunting engines used in marshalling yards to the 40-metre-long, 350-ton 'Big Boy' locomotives used in the USA to pull long-distance goods trains at speeds up to 115kph.

The tender carried coal or wood for the fire, and water tanks to top up the boiler.

Automatic control

The steam engine's speed was controlled by a mechanism called a governor. Two heavy iron balls were spun round by the engine. If the machine ran too fast, the whirling force (page 18) made the balls fly upwards and pull levers to shut off the supply of steam.

If the engine runs too fast

The balls rise

Levers pull upwards

The chain pulls the steam valve shut and slows the engine.

If the engine slows down

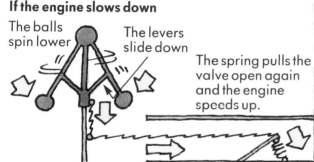

The balls spin lower

The levers slide down

The spring pulls the valve open again and the engine speeds up.

Believe it or not – it's a car. This weird-looking contraption was built in France in 1770. It was driven by steam and was the first real machine-powered road vehicle. It could travel at about 3kph.

Did you know ... the world land speed record was once held by a steam-driven car? The American 'Rocket' topped 200kph and broke the world record in 1906.

Steam-powered fairground traction engines were used to pull caravans, and were fitted with generators to make electricity for the fairground lights. You can still see them at fairs and country fetes.

Steam collects in the dome and is led from there to the cylinders by pipes running through the boiler.

Each 'chuff' of a steam engine is made by a blast of used steam from the cylinders being forced up the blast pipe. The draught sucks hot air from the firebox through the fire tubes and these heat the water in the main boiler.

CHIMNEY

USED STEAM FROM THE CYLINDERS

SAFETY VALVE

SMOKEBOX

FIRE TUBES FULL OF HOT GASES

BLAST PIPE

CONNECTING RODS

DRIVING WHEEL

CYLINDER

Up, up and away

If you hold a sheet of paper close to your bottom lip and blow across the top of it, you might expect it to be pushed downwards. But just the opposite happens. The paper rises, and stays up as long as you keep blowing. This gives a clue to how birds and aeroplanes fly.

Whenever air rushes over a curved surface, like the upper surface of a wing, it speeds up. And the faster the air moves, the less it presses on the surface it is flowing over. With low pressure above the wing and higher pressure underneath, the wing is pushed upwards. Aero-engineers call this force 'lift'. It is caused simply by the air rushing over the wing, yet it can lift anything from a sparrow to a 400-tonne Jumbo jet.

BLOW ACROSS THE PAPER

FAST MOVING AIR = LOW PRESSURE

LIFT

STILL AIR = HIGHER PRESSURE

Spot the aerofoils
Lots of natural and man-made flying things have the special aerofoil shape. See how many you can think of. (There are some clues at the bottom of the page.)

A working aerofoil

1 5CM 8CM 7CM
2
3
4
5 THREAD LIFT PIN HOLES

Take a piece of stiff paper 15cm × 5cm and make a fold 8cm from one end (1). Place the long side under a ruler (2) and pull gently upwards. This will give it a nice even curve (3). Tape the edges

together (4) to make the special aerofoil shape. If you thread some cotton through holes in the wing, stretch it tight, then blow at the leading edge of the wing, you will be able to fly it up the thread.

Build and test-fly your own glider

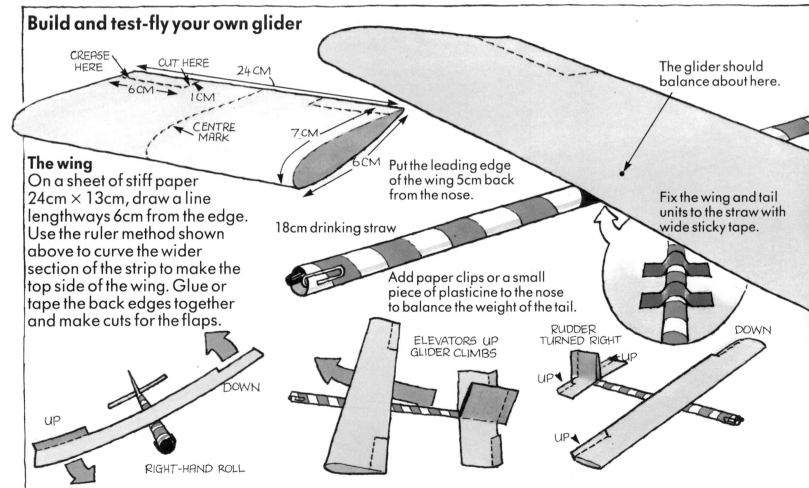

CREASE HERE CUT HERE 24 CM
6CM 1CM
CENTRE MARK 7CM 6CM

The glider should balance about here.

Put the leading edge of the wing 5cm back from the nose.

18cm drinking straw

Fix the wing and tail units to the straw with wide sticky tape.

Add paper clips or a small piece of plasticine to the nose to balance the weight of the tail.

The wing
On a sheet of stiff paper 24cm × 13cm, draw a line lengthways 6cm from the edge. Use the ruler method shown above to curve the wider section of the strip to make the top side of the wing. Glue or tape the back edges together and make cuts for the flaps.

DOWN
UP
RIGHT-HAND ROLL

ELEVATORS UP GLIDER CLIMBS

RUDDER TURNED RIGHT
UP UP DOWN UP

Rolling in flight
You can make the glider roll in flight by moving the wing flaps (ailerons) like this. Always move one aileron up and the other down.

Climbing and diving
The tail-plane elevators are used to make the glider climb or dive. Unlike the ailerons, the elevators both move in the same direction.

Making a turn
A right-hand turn uses ailerons and rudder together like this. The elevators are turned up slightly to keep the glider's nose up.

30

A bird's wing-feather, a bird's wing, a boomerang, a sycamore seed, a Frisbee, a hang-glider.

Sailing into the wind

Old square-rigged sailing ships could only sail when the wind was behind them, pushing them along. But a modern yacht can sail in any direction, even into a head-wind. Does this bird's-eye view tell you how this is possible?

Does this shape remind you of anything?

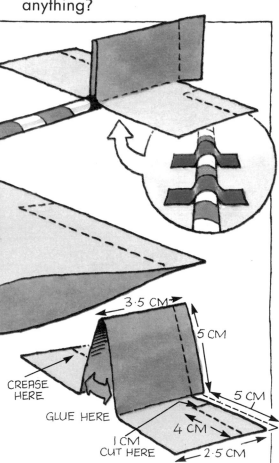

3·5 CM

5 CM

5 CM

4 CM

2·5 CM

CREASE HERE

GLUE HERE

1 CM CUT HERE

The tail

Take a piece of stiff paper 20cm × 3.5cm and fold it like this. Cut away the back 1cm of the tail planes so that the upright rudder is left sticking out. Make cuts for the elevator flaps and crease the paper along the dotted lines.

How helicopters fly

Instead of rushing along a runway to get enough lift for take-off, the helicopter stands still and makes its 'wings' rush through the air instead. The rotor blades are long narrow aerofoils, and the faster they spin, the more lift they make. The helicopter is steered by tilting the rotor unit in the direction you want to go. Because helicopters can hover, and land almost anywhere, they are used for rescue work and for lifting men on and off oil-rigs.

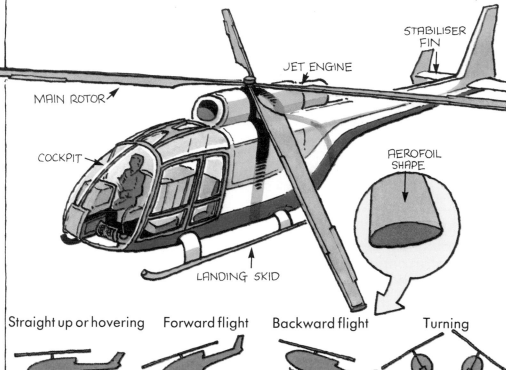

STABILISER FIN

JET ENGINE

MAIN ROTOR

COCKPIT

AEROFOIL SHAPE

LANDING SKID

Straight up or hovering   Forward flight   Backward flight   Turning

Hold your own helicopter championship

The drawings on page 36 show you how to make the main rotor for a model helicopter. All you need for your test flight is a pencil, and a fine day without too much wind. Wind your launching string round the bobbin, and slip the bobbin on to the pencil. Tilt the helicopter slightly in the direction you want to fly, then launch it with a smooth steady pull on the string. See how far and how high you can fly.

You can experiment by changing the amount of twist and droop on your rotor blades.

Heating up and cooling down

Whenever a solid object is heated it gets bigger. Scientists say it has 'expanded'. Some things expand more than others. Metals, for example, expand quite a lot when they are heated and this can cause problems for engineers. A big iron bridge like the Forth railway bridge is more than a metre longer on hot summer days than it is in winter when the metal is cool. Concrete bridges expand too, and if you look carefully at a motorway fly-over you will see there are small gaps in the road to leave room for the bridge to expand without causing damage.

Even people expand on hot days. That is why your shoes feel tight.

The famous Forth railway bridge can expand by more than a metre in summer.

Blackpool tower can 'grow' more than 3cm on a very hot day.

The expanding rod experiment

This experiment is easy to do, but like all experiments that use flames it should only be done when there are grown-ups about. Set up the experiment like this and see how much a steel knitting needle expands. Try the experiment with rods of other metals. Do they expand by the same amount? If not, which metal expands the most?

Let everything cool down for 15 minutes after you have blown out the candles. The metal gets very hot.

The expanding rod rolls the needle along and the pointer magnifies the tiny movement so it is easier to see.

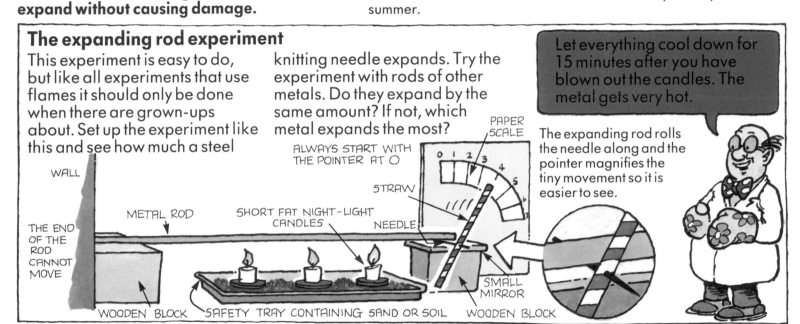

ALWAYS START WITH THE POINTER AT O

PAPER SCALE

STRAW

NEEDLE

WALL

THE END OF THE ROD CANNOT MOVE

METAL ROD

SHORT FAT NIGHT-LIGHT CANDLES

SMALL MIRROR

WOODEN BLOCK

WOODEN BLOCK SAFETY TRAY CONTAINING SAND OR SOIL

Putting expansion to work

If two strips, made of different metals, are joined together and then heated, the one that expands most will bend the strip into a curve. This can be used to turn an electrical circuit on and off. This kind of switch is used to control the temperature of an iron, and to control central heating systems.

Cold
The strip is straight

Hot
This side expands a little

This side expands more and bends the strip

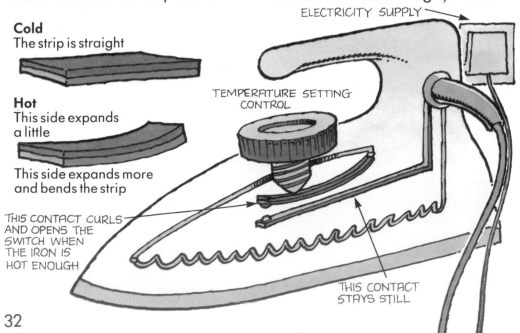

ELECTRICITY SUPPLY

TEMPERATURE SETTING CONTROL

THIS CONTACT CURLS AND OPENS THE SWITCH WHEN THE IRON IS HOT ENOUGH

THIS CONTACT STAYS STILL

A handy household tip

Next time your Mum or Dad cannot get the top off a jar, help them with simple science. Hold the jar top under the hot tap for a few seconds — then unscrew it (using a cloth).

Can you explain why the top comes off so easily?

Floating on air

Gases expand too when they get hot, and this makes them lighter so they float upwards. (You can test this by holding a piece of tissue over a hot radiator. The rising hot air makes the tissue flutter.) Page 37 shows you how to make a hot air balloon. Here is how to make the heater, and how to launch the balloon.

Hot air balloons work best on cold days when there is no wind. You could organise a balloon championship among your friends at school.

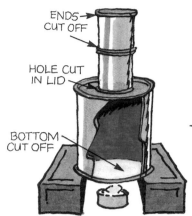

ENDS CUT OFF

HOLE CUT IN LID

BOTTOM CUT OFF

The heater chimney is made from a paint tin and two food tins. These need to be cut and joined together, so ask a grown-up to do this bit. Beware of sharp edges.

The heater is a small tin containing a wad of cotton wool soaked in methylated spirit (meths). Stand the chimney on some bricks, with the heater underneath.

Light the meths, then hold the balloon over the chimney but do not let it touch the hot metal. The balloon will fill with hot air until it is light enough to lift off.

Free hot water

Here is a good experiment for a hot summer day. Fill the hosepipe with water, turn off the tap, and leave the hose in the sun for a few hours. Then unfasten the tap connector and let the water in the pipe run into a basin.

Dark-coloured plastic pipes work best.

Test the water carefully. You will be surprised how hot it can get.

Keeping things cool

As you dry in the sun after a swim, the water on your body turns to vapour. But it needs heat to make the change – and it takes some of that heat from your body. That is why you feel cooler. Fridges work the same way. The pipes you see behind the fridge contain freon, a substance that can turn from a liquid to a vapour, and back again, very easily. Each time it changes it either takes in heat or gives out heat. Follow the freon round the pipes and see how it works.

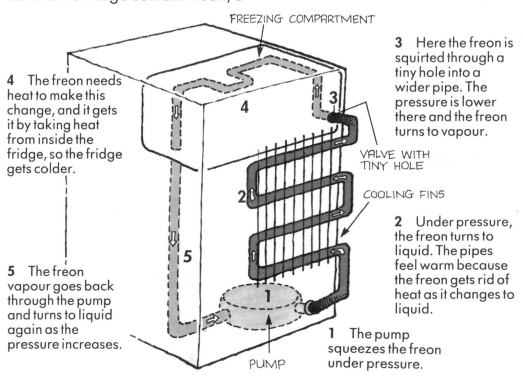

FREEZING COMPARTMENT

3 Here the freon is squirted through a tiny hole into a wider pipe. The pressure is lower there and the freon turns to vapour.

VALVE WITH TINY HOLE

COOLING FINS

4 The freon needs heat to make this change, and it gets it by taking heat from inside the fridge, so the fridge gets colder.

5 The freon vapour goes back through the pump and turns to liquid again as the pressure increases.

2 Under pressure, the freon turns to liquid. The pipes feel warm because the freon gets rid of heat as it changes to liquid.

1 The pump squeezes the freon under pressure.

PUMP

Jets and rockets

If you accidentally drop the hose pipe while spraying the garden, you should grab it again quickly or run for cover. Instead of just lying there the hose will wriggle and jump about, squirting water in all directions. The hose pipe is obeying one of the laws of physics. This law says that for every force there is an equal force pushing in the opposite direction. So, as water squirts from the hose, the nozzle tries to jump backwards in the opposite direction. The same thing happens when a hunter fires his gun. As the bullet shoots from the barrel the gun jerks back against the hunter's shoulder. We call this force the 'recoil', and we use it in many machines, from garden sprinklers to jet engines.

Supersonic jet-power

The huge turbojet engines that power Concorde use exactly the same idea as the simple balloon jet shown above. Hot gases roar from the jet nozzles, and the recoil drives the aircraft forward through the air. The amount of recoil force (called thrust) that the engine can make depends on how much fuel it burns, and that depends on how much air it can suck in. So jet engines have big compressors at the front that force air into the engine at high pressure. Concorde can fly at twice the speed of sound.

Experiments with recoil

Does the recoil change if you use different-sized pebbles?

For safety, try this experiment out of doors. Set up a simple catapult gun like this, mounted on rollers, then fire it by cutting the thread. Watch what happens to the gun platform.

See how far you can fly a home-made balloon jet. The compressed air squirts from the jet nozzle and the recoil sends the balloon shooting along the guide line, just like a real jet engine.

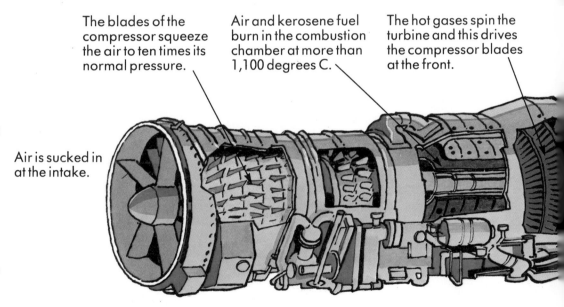

The blades of the compressor squeeze the air to ten times its normal pressure.

Air and kerosene fuel burn in the combustion chamber at more than 1,100 degrees C.

The hot gases spin the turbine and this drives the compressor blades at the front.

Air is sucked in at the intake.

All this talk about jets should help you explain why the sprinkler spins round without a motor.

The fastest thing on wheels

In October 1983, Englishman Richard Noble drove his jet-powered car *Thrust 2* across the mud-flats of Black Rock Desert in America at 1,019.4kph (633.5mph). It was a new world land speed record.

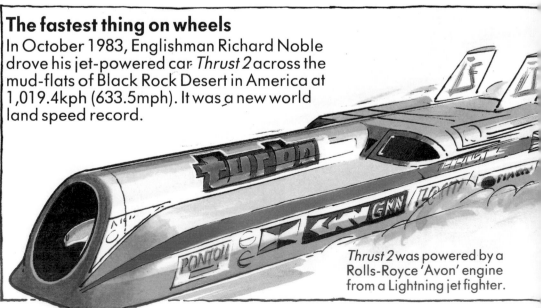

Thrust 2 was powered by a Rolls-Royce 'Avon' engine from a Lightning jet fighter.

You can make a steam-powered jet boat from a metal cigar tube or tablet tube. But candles and hot water can be dangerous, so take great care and ask a grown-up to help with the experiment.

METAL TUBE
SCREW CAP
CANDLE
SMALL HOLE MADE WITH A THIN NAIL
WIRE SUPPORTS
STEAM JET
PUT 2-3 TEASPOONS OF WATER INSIDE THE TUBE
BALSA WOOD BOAT

The gases are then forced out through the jet nozzle to produce the engine's powerful thrust.

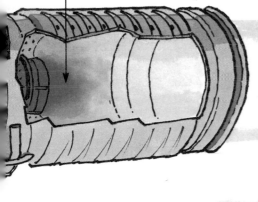

The car had a smooth aluminium skin to reduce the drag caused by friction with the air.

Next stop – the Moon

The Saturn V launch vehicle that carried American astronauts to the Moon was more than 110m tall and weighed as much as a loaded 70-truck goods train.

The huge first-stage rocket contained more than 2,000 tons of fuel, but it burned for only 2½ minutes before the second-stage rocket took over. By the time the third-stage rocket had burned out, the astronauts' capsule was hurtling through space at 11km a second.

Nothing can burn without oxygen, and as there is no oxygen beyond the Earth's atmosphere, space rockets have to carry their own supply. Without it they could not burn their rocket fuel. That is why nearly all the room inside the huge Saturn launch vehicle is taken up by tanks of fuel and liquid oxygen.

Who needs a runway?

The jet nozzles of the Harrier's engines can swivel to change the direction of thrust. By pointing them straight down, the aircraft can take off and land vertically. Once in the air, the nozzles are swivelled to point backwards and the Harrier can roar away in normal level flight.

Level flight

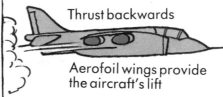

Thrust backwards

Aerofoil wings provide the aircraft's lift

Take-off and landing

Thrust downwards

Recoil provides the aircraft's lift

In an emergency the escape rocket snatches the capsule away from the launch rocket and drops it by parachute a safe distance away.

Space capsule

Lunar module

Third-stage rocket
Final speed 11km/sec

Liquid hydrogen

Liquid oxygen

1 rocket motor

Second-stage rocket
Final speed 7km/sec

Liquid hydrogen

Liquid oxygen

5 rocket motors

First-stage rocket
Final speed 2.7km/sec

Liquid oxygen

Paraffin fuel

The bell-shaped jet nozzles of the first-stage rocket stood twice as high as a man.

5 rocket motors

Stabilizing fins

35

The helicopter rotor

For the rotor you will need tracing paper, a pencil and ruler, scissors, glue, a light plastic cotton reel and a square of card about 20cm × 20cm (the back of a cereal packet works well). Lay the tracing paper on this page and trace the shape of the rotor. Make sure you trace the dotted fold lines as well. Scribble on the back of the tracing and transfer the shape to the plain side of your card. You can decorate it later with coloured pens — it will be the top side of the rotor. Cut out the shape of the rotor.

INSTEAD OF TRACING THE SHAPE YOU COULD DRAW IT OUT USING THE MEASUREMENTS ON THIS PATTERN

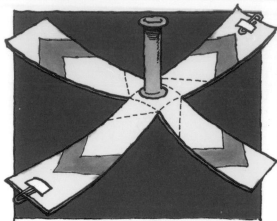

3. Tape a small weight, such as a paper clip or button, to the tips of one pair of blades as shown.

$2\frac{1}{2}$ CM

$1\frac{1}{4}$ CM

$2\frac{1}{2}$ CM

9 CM (YOU CAN EXPERIMENT WITH DIFFERENT LENGTHS)

$1\frac{1}{4}$ CM

$3\frac{1}{2}$ CM

$2\frac{1}{2}$ CM

1. Turn the rotor over and glue the cotton reel to the card, making sure that it is in the centre.

4. The rotor will look like this from the side. The slight twist and droop helps the blades bite into the air as they spin.

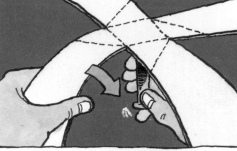

2. Carefully bend the rotor blades along the dotted lines, and bend them down slightly along the lines of the centre square.

Always wind the string towards the high edge of the rotor blades or the helicopter will try to take off downwards instead of up.

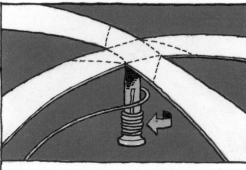

5. Wind a length of thin string round the reel so that it traps the loose end as shown here. Make 12 to 15 complete turns.

The hot air balloon

You will need a pencil and ruler, a stapler, glue, some newspaper, and twelve standard sheets of tissue paper joined in pairs along the short side to give six sheets roughly 50cm wide and 140cm long.

Fold the sheets in half so that the long edges meet. Then stack the folded sheets in a pile and staple the unfolded edges as shown.

Draw lines 5cm apart along and across the top sheet in the stack. Use this grid to copy the shape on the 1-cm grid opposite. Cut out the shape, cutting through all the sheets together.

Put some newspaper inside the first folded panel, then run a thin line of glue along the edge of the tissue paper. Place the next panel on top and press down along the edge.

Place newspaper inside the next panel, to stop any glue soaking through, then glue and position the next panel. Repeat until all six sheets are joined together.

This is the tricky bit. When the glue is dry, open up the concertina folds and glue the last two edges together to complete the balloon.

Finally, use a hair drier to blow up the balloon. This will not make it fly but it helps the glue dry and gives the balloon its proper shape, ready for the big launch.

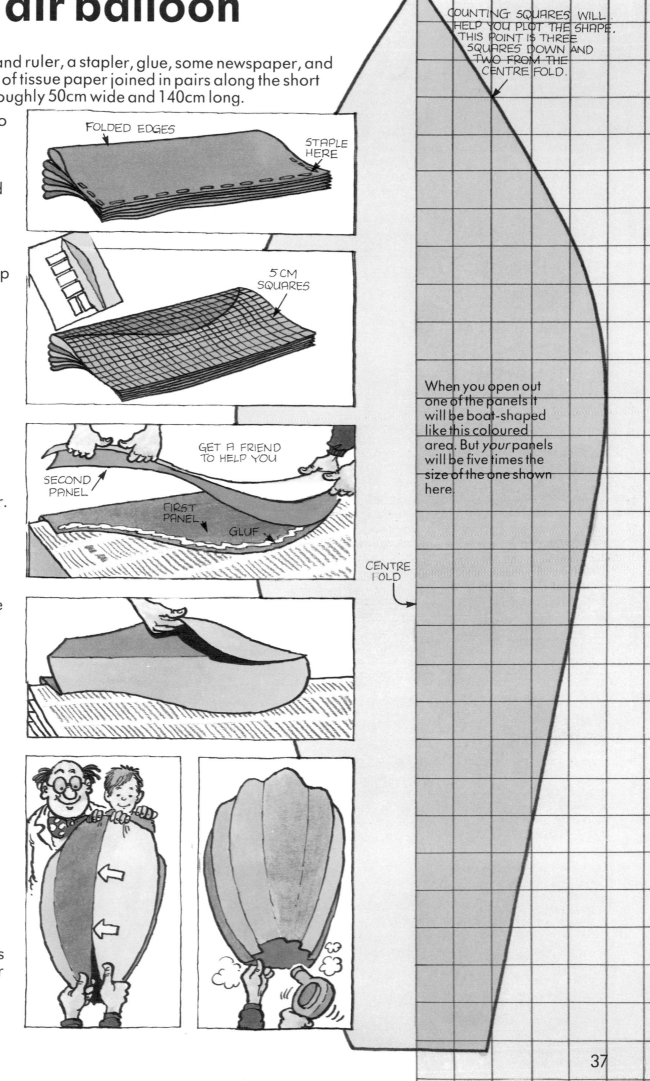

FOLDED EDGES

STAPLE HERE

5 CM SQUARES

GET A FRIEND TO HELP YOU

SECOND PANEL

FIRST PANEL

GLUE

COUNTING SQUARES WILL HELP YOU PLOT THE SHAPE. THIS POINT IS THREE SQUARES DOWN AND TWO FROM THE CENTRE FOLD.

When you open out one of the panels it will be boat-shaped like this coloured area. But *your* panels will be five times the size of the one shown here.

CENTRE FOLD

37

Index